DISNEY's
THE LITTLE MERMAID

The official movie adaptation

Walt Disney Publications, Inc.
Burbank, California

Adapted from
Walt Disney Pictures'
The Little Mermaid

Produced by
Howard Ashman
and
John Musker

Written and directed by
John Musker
and
Ron Clements

Based on the fairy tale by
Hans Christian Andersen

AND *NOW*, FOLKS, GRACING TONIGHT'S CONCERT WITH HIS AUGUST PRESENCE--

--HIS ROYAL HIGHNESS--

TRA-TRA-TERRAH!

--KING TRITON!

HOORAY! LONG LIVE THE KING!!

NEXT, PRESENTING THE DISTINGUISHED COURT COMPOSER--

--HORATIO FELONIOUS IGNACIOUS CRUSTACEOUS *SEBASTIAN!*

7

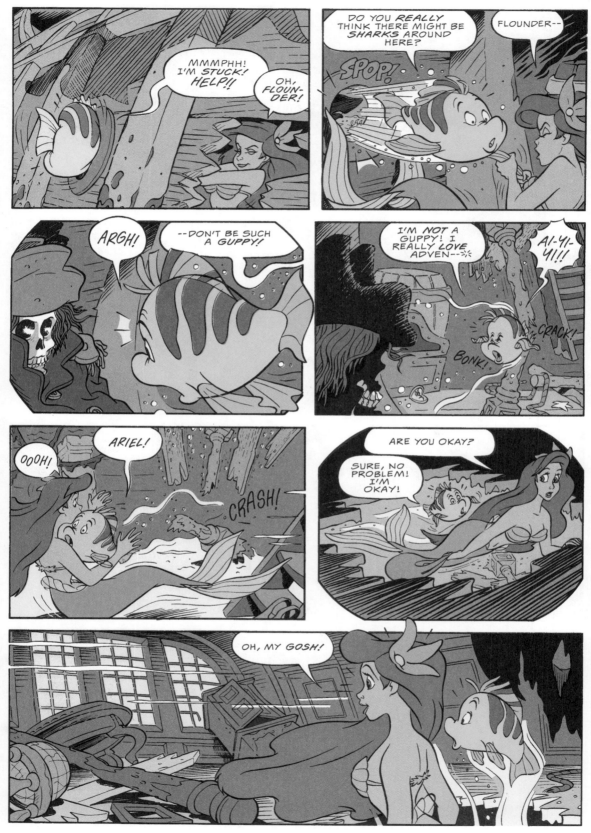

8

WHUPS! HERE *ALREADY?* WHAT A SWIM!

SCUTTLE! LOOK WHAT *WE* FOUND!

WE WERE IN THIS SUNKEN *SHIP*, SEE-- IT WAS REALLY *CREEPY!*

HUMAN STUFF, HUH?

LOOK AT THIS--NOW THIS IS *SPECIAL*-- THIS IS *VERY UNUSUAL!*

WHAT? WHAT IS IT?

IT'S A *DINGELHOPPER!* HUMANS USE THESE LITTLE BABIES TO STRAIGHTEN THEIR *HAIR* OUT!

A LITTLE TWIRL HERE AND A YANK THERE AND *VIOLA*, YA GETS AN ESTHETICALLY-PLEASING CONFIGURATION OF *HAIR!*

A *DINGEL-HOPPER!*

WHAT ABOUT *THAT* ONE?

THIS IS A BANDED, BULBOUS-- UH-- *SNARFBLATT*, DATING BACK TO *PRE-HYSTERICAL* TIMES!

HUMANS INVENTED THE SNARFBLATT TO MAKE FINE *MUSIC!*

ALLOW ME...

MUSIC!

THE *CONCERT!* OH, MY GOSH! MY FATHER'S GOING TO *KILL* ME!

THE CONCERT WAS *TODAY?!*

EH?

I JUST DON'T *SEE* THINGS THE WAY DADDY DOES! A WORLD THAT MAKES SUCH WONDERFUL THINGS *CAN'T* BE BAD!

BUT IT ISN'T JUST *THINGS* I WANT! IT'S BEING WHERE THE *PEOPLE* LIVE!

I'D GIVE ANYTHING TO *LIVE* UP THERE, BREATHING THE AIR AND GOING ANY-WHERE I *PLEASED!*

OOPS!

HOW I'D *LOVE* TO LIVE IN THAT WORLD SOMEDAY!

SEBASTIAN!

POP!

ARGH!

ARIEL, WHAT ARE YOU-- AH, HOW *COULD* YOU--EH-- WHAT *IS* ALL DIS??

JUST MY *COLLECTION!*

HEY THERE, KIDDO! QUITE A SHOW, HUH?

OH, SCUTTLE! I'VE NEVER SEEN A HUMAN THIS CLOSE BEFORE!

=SIGH!= HE'S VERY HANDSOME, ISN'T HE?

WOOF!

I DUNNO--

--HE LOOKS KINDA HAIRY AND SLOBBERY TO ME!

NOT THAT ONE-- THE ONE PLAYING THE SNARFBLATT!

SILENCE! SILENCE!

IT IS NOW MY HONOR AND PRIVILEGE TO PRESENT OUR ESTEEMED PRINCE ERIC WITH A VERY SPECIAL, VERY EXPEN- SIVE--

--VERY LARGE BIRTHDAY PRESENT!

AW, GRIMSBY, YOU OLD BEANPOLE-- YOU SHOULDN'T HAVE!

I KNOW!

HAPPY BIRTH- DAY, ERIC!

AW, GEE, GRIM! IT'S... UMM.... IT'S REALLY SOMETHING!

GRR!

OF COURSE, I HAD HOPED IT WOULD BE A WEDDING PRESENT, BUT--

C'MON, GRIM... DON'T START!

YOU'RE NOT STILL SORE BECAUSE I DIDN'T FALL FOR THE PRINCESS OF GLOWERHAVEN, ARE YOU?

IT ISN'T ME ALONE! THE ENTIRE KINGDOM WANTS TO SEE YOU HAPPILY SETTLED DOWN WITH THE RIGHT GIRL!

23

24

33

36

40

42

43